SPECTACLES
ANN BEATTIE

ILLUSTRATED BY WINSLOW PELS

ARIEL BOOKS
WORKMAN PUBLISHING, NEW YORK

Library of Congress Cataloging in Publication Data

Beattie, Ann.
   Spectacles.
   (Goblin tales)
   Summary: When Alison puts on Great Grandmother's
glasses, they become magical and enable her to understand
some of her great grandmother's frustrations and
unfulfilled aspirations.
   [1. Grandmothers—Fiction.   2. Old age—Fiction.
3. Eyeglasses—Fiction]   I. Pels, Winslow,
1947- ill.   II. Title.   III. Series
PZ7.B380527Sp 1985   [Fic]   85-15088
ISBN 0-89480-926-1

Workman Publishing Company
1 West 39th Street
New York, N.Y. 10018

Manufactured in the United States of America
First printing September 1985
        10   9   8   7   6   5   4   3   2   1

SPECTACLES

ALISON GOT WONDERFUL PRESENTS for her birthday: a punching bag in the shape of a clown, and a very warm bedcover puffed up with down; a mirror ringed with lights in which she could pose, striped knee-socks, a polka-dot blouse, and a straw hat with a rose.

Nicholas brought a bird that sang when you turned the key
Tess brought a china set to serve your dolls tea;
Andy brought candy (though he ate it himself)
Susan brought colored pencils (and a drawing of an elf);
Her aunt sent a card that said, "Now you're eight!"
From Tom Z., she got a globe to inflate;
Priscilla brought ribbons to tie at your throat
Claire brought pink heart-shaped soap that would float;
Bill brought a record by a Brazilian band
Lynn brought a flashlight you could hide in your hand;
Will brought a stopwatch ("See how fast you can run!")
Jay brought a kite in the shape of the sun
Devon brought brownies that still needed to bake (not quite done).

Alison enjoyed her birthday party, too, even though her mother did not spend every minute in the room while the party was going on. Alison's Great

Grandmother, who had come to visit, had arrived the day before the party and had gotten sick. She slept through the party, and Alison's mother left often to check on her.

Now that the party was over and everyone had gone home, though, Alison began to feel sorry for herself. She wasn't getting any attention at all, and it was her birthday. She picked up the crumpled paper and the ribbons and took them to the trash. When she looked at her presents again, even that made her feel a little sorry for herself. There was no wind, so she couldn't fly the kite. She wasn't sure how to turn on the stereo, so she couldn't listen to her new record. She liked the colored pencils, but she would never be able to draw as well as Susan.

She climbed the stairs to the bedroom where Great Grandmother was resting. The door was open a crack, so she peeked in and then quietly opened the door. The curtains were drawn, and Great Grandmother was napping. Her mother was sitting in a chair, with a small lamp shining on her book. When she saw Alison, she gestured for her to go back into the hallway. Then she got up and followed her out.

"What is it?" her mother whispered.

"Everybody went home," Alison said. "I don't have anything to do."

Her mother frowned and shook her head. "If you don't have anything to do after getting all those presents . . ."

"Put on the record for me," Alison said.

"In a minute," her mother said. "I'm going to spend a little more time in Great Grandma's room."

"You have to come down anyway, to take the brownies out of the oven."

"Not for five more minutes," her mother said, looking at her watch.

"Is that Alison?" Great Grandmother called.

Alison and her mother went into the room. Great Grandma was sitting up in bed. She had had the flu, and now she was weak and dizzy.

"When does everyone come for the birthday party?" she said.

"They already came," Alison said.

"I didn't hear them. Why didn't you wake me up?"

"Because you needed your sleep," Alison's mother said. "How are you feeling now?"

"I feel like I missed the party," Great Grandmother said.

"I'm going to take the brownies out," Alison's mother said. "Do you want brownies or birthday cake?"

"Both," Great Grandmother said.

"I guess you *are* feeling better!"

"Come and tell me about your presents," Great Grandmother said.

Alison sat on the bed, but she wished she didn't have to tell Great Grandmother about her gifts. Whenever people told Great Grandmother that something was terrible she said it was nice, but whenever something was clearly wonderful — like all the presents — Great Grandmother acted grumpy and disagreed whenever she could.

The bed Alison sat on had belonged to Great Grandmother before she gave it to Alison's parents. It was kept in the guest room, but lately Great Grandmother had been ill so often that she spent a lot of time in the room, and it had almost become her room now. It was a tester bed, with a white canopy patterned with stars. Alison loved to sit on the bed and look up. When her mother put the blue sheets on the bed, she felt like she was floating in the sky.

"I got a bird that hops when you wind it with a key," Alison said.

"When *I* was young, " Great Grandmother said, "people had brass bird-cages with real canaries."

"And I got a globe that you blow up, like a beach ball."

"I wish you had gotten a trip around the world," Great Grandmother said.

Music started playing downstairs. Alison's mother had put on her new record.

"That's music from Brazil," Alison said.

"If we were in Brazil, we could see the smiling faces of the musicians,"

16

Great Grandmother said. "It's warm there, so we'd be outside, dancing on a terrace, with lemon trees and hibiscus growing all around us."

"You could wear the hat with the rose I got for my birthday," Alison said.

"Is it a real rose?"

"It's made out of silk."

"I'm sure it's pretty," Great Grandmother said, "but what makes real roses so wonderful is the way they smell."

Alison was getting frustrated. According to Great Grandmother, nothing was ever good enough. Things were always better the way they might be or the way they used to be.

"Don't you like anything the way it is?" Alison said.

Great Grandmother looked surprised. "I like many things the way they are," she said, "but I guess that sometimes the things I remember are better now than they really were." She leaned toward Alison. "One of the advantages to being old is that when you talk about the past to people who weren't

there with you, they believe what you say. You can make everything seem
wonderful, if you want to."

Great Grandmother remembered:

> *A snowman Great Grandfather made, with a scarf at its throat*
> *A sand castle, with seashell windows, surrounded by a moat;*
> *A carriage ride through snow in Central Park*
> *Seeing an eclipse — the moon growing dark;*
> *Mr. Barkin's dog, that dived for rocks.*
> *Being in bed with chicken pox;*
> *The nest her brother took down from a tree*
> *Seeing a beehive — but not the queen bee;*
> *In the museum, a jeweled Fabergé egg*
> *At the zoo, a flamingo that stood on one leg;*
> *Peach ice cream, studded with fruit*
> *That it once was in fashion to wear a zoot suit.*

Alison's mother came into the room with a glass of juice and a plate on a
tray. There was a brownie and a piece of cake on the plate.

Great Grandmother took a bite of the brownie. "Mmm, thank you," she
said. "And that's the thing, Alison: you never remember or imagine *exactly*,
even if you think you do."

"Then how can you be sure that everything can be so much better?"

"Alison!" her mother said, shocked.

"It's a fair question," Great Grandmother said. "I guess I have to admit that I complain a lot. It's because I'm mad at myself, you know — because even then I didn't have enough fun. I let so many things get in my way."

"How can you say that?" Alison's mother said. "You were always busy, and most of the time you were certainly having fun."

Alison's mother remembered:

> Her Grandmother making pies, fluting the edge with her thumb
> That Grandfather would sing, Grandmother would hum;
> Earrings fashioned for her out of bing cherries
> Bedtime stories with pictures of kings, queens and faeries;
> Grandmother on a ladder, painting the porch ceiling blue
> (It was a mystery who did it; Grandfather didn't have a clue).

"Busy doesn't mean you're doing the right things," Great Grandmother said. "What would it have mattered if a little dust stayed? And if all my famous dinners had been only half as good, I could have spent more time outside, walking in the world."

"DADDY," ALISON SAID as he tucked her in bed, "do you let things get in your way?"

"What do you mean?" he said.

"Great Grandma said she didn't do a lot of things she wanted because things got in her way."

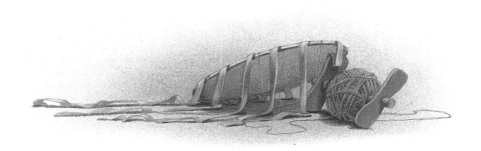

"You can't go through life without things getting in your way. They built a skyscraper beside my office, and *that's* in my way. I look out expecting to see clouds, and I see people sitting at their desks, just like me. A moving van blocked the intersection on my way home tonight. *That* was in my way."

Alison's mother stood in the doorway. "Come on — she's asking you a serious question," she said.

"*This* is in the way of my giving you a hug goodnight," her father said, giving her a squeeze through the thick down bedcover.

"He does," Alison's mother said, coming into the room to hug her. "We all do."

Alison's father was muttering as he left the room. "That moving van pulled into the middle of the intersection on a yellow light," he said. "Where are the traffic cops when we need them?"

"Great Grandma's feeling a little sorry for herself because she's sick," Alison's mother said. "You know how much you complain yourself, when you don't feel well."

"Doesn't she really wish that she'd gone to Brazil?" Alison said.

"I'm sure part of her wishes that. But you know, it's also nice just to wish for things. When you only wish for them and don't have them, the things can stay the same. When you get what you wish for, things can go wrong."

Her mother kissed her and left the room, and Alison closed her eyes.

THE METAL BIRD HEARD what Alison's mother said and remembered its past: What would it like, if it could have a wish?

As a real bird, it had to peck and peck at the ground to pull out worms. It had to sit on its nest through rainstorms, and it had to fly long distances to go south for the winter and to return in the spring. Life as a toy bird had its advantages, but the only thing it missed was hearing its own song whenever it wished. The thing the bird would most like would be to sing whenever it wanted again, without being wound.

The painted metal feathers suddenly ruffled, and the wings painted on the bird extended. It flapped its wings and flew to the top of a lamp, and perched there. It began to sing. It sang and sang, and was so involved in its song that it barely had time to fly away when the cat that crept across the floor was about to pounce.

It would be nice to be a singing bird again — but it would have to remember to stay very alert.

The ribbons Priscilla had brought rustled with thought.

They'd rather be larger, and a more interesting shape: banners, blowing in the wind.

The silver ribbon that held all the others tied in a figure-8 untied itself, and all the ribbons flew up to a corner of the room and began to flap proudly in the breeze.

But it got tiring, having to ripple and snap and wave high. They began to think that being woven through a braid, or being tied in a neat little bow under the collar of a blouse, would be easier. And when they were bows, they got to hear the compliments. High up, they heard only the sound of the wind.

What about it, the punching-bag clown thought.
To perform again, pirouetting and prancing in a circus.
To juggle and dance
And give kicks in the pants
To upstage an acrobat and collide with a roller-skating bear
All the nonsense made it such fun to be there

ALISON OPENED HER EYES AGAIN. She was thinking of too many things to sleep. She got out of bed and walked quietly to her door. The house was dark. Her mother and father had gone to bed early. She could hear the faint music of the radio in their bedroom (actually, it was the metal bird, concentrating on singing very, very quietly so the cat wouldn't wake up). She went to the pile of boxes and found the little flashlight, then lit the way downstairs, to the kitchen, the circles of white moving in front of her feet.

She wanted some brownies. They were on the counter, in a pan, with foil stretched across the top. As she came closer, she saw that a knife was in the sink, and a plate. Someone had already been eating brownies. She unwrapped the pan and cut herself a long strip of brownies, then sat at the table to eat them.

That was where she saw the oval, gold-rimmed glasses. Great Grandmother's glasses. That was who had come downstairs to eat more brownies.

Alison ate the brownies, then washed and dried her plate and put it back on the shelf, so that no one would know that she had crept downstairs. She tried on the glasses. Everything looked blurry and strange. She kept them on, though, to see what it would be like to walk through the house with them on. Looking down, the stairs seemed more like pools of water than steps. The rug was out of focus, so that she couldn't quite see the pattern; it looked like a long, soft stretch of beach. She was still wearing the glasses when she tiptoed into her room. Great Grandmother always got up later than she did. She could put them back on the counter in the morning.

But where to hide them until then?

She went again to her pile of birthday presents and decided to open the lid of the top box and put the glasses in there, with the tissue paper, so that they would be safe. She took off the lid and put the glasses in the box. A little light shone through the side of the window, where the shade did not fit tight against the window frame. It shone over the box, and over one lens of the glasses. It looked as if one lens was blinking, as she started to step away. She had only to move her head back a foot, and the lens was dark; a foot forward, and it was bright. She did this a few times, moving her head into and out of the light, and then she reached for the winking glasses. She thought that she would look one more time at her room in the soft focus.

Things were blurry, but that wasn't what surprised her. What surprised her was that it wasn't her room. Everything was different. She turned and looked to the side. The windows were covered with lace curtains instead of white shades. They looked like large Valentine cards. Alison looked at the floor. It was covered with a rose-colored carpet, and on the walls — her pink-painted walls — was wallpaper patterned with tiny flowers. The bed was not a bed. In its place was a large sofa with a high back and high, rolling arms, and on the sofa — she was squinting hard now — on the sofa sat two people, turned toward each other, their knees almost touching. It was too strange, and she started to take the glasses off, but as she began to take them away from her eyes, the man on the sofa leaned a little toward the woman, as if he meant to speak. He froze, lips parted, until Alison pushed the glasses back up on her nose. Then he leaned forward slowly, and took one of the woman's hands in his. The woman turned her head toward him and Alison realized, from her profile, that it was her Great Grandmother. But this was a great grandmother she had seen only in photographs: she wore a long dress that touched the floor, and only the pointed toes of her shoes were visible. Her hair was not white but auburn, coiled in a bun at the back of her neck. The dress had a high collar, edged in lace, that rose almost to her chin. It was difficult to hear what the man was saying, because he was murmuring. Alison moved forward, but both figures froze, as if they had heard.

Alison was as still as the metal bird, and as silent. She willed her own heart to be quiet — as still as the little heart-shaped soaps in the box on the floor. The punching bag clown stood silent watch with her.

After a few seconds, the man began to speak again, and the woman moved her head closer to his, to listen. It seemed that he was offering something. Alison could see that her Great Grandmother was perplexed. The man continued to speak, but if her Great Grandmother had not finally spoken, just a bit louder than the man, Alison would not have been able to make out what they were talking about. "I think you are quite wonderful," her Great Grandmother said. "It isn't necessary to offer me the stars."

Now the man dropped his eyes, and the woman began to laugh, softly. She held out her other hand, and the man took it. It was so quiet that all Alison could hear was the clock ticking in the room.

The clown was pleased that he had guessed what was going on from the first. He had seen those looks before, at the circus: the man with four arms,

who loved the lady with two heads; the baboon who fell in love with a silver spoon.

Plans were being made by Alison's Great Grandmother. Roses. There was going to be an altar banked with roses. She would wear a long, white lace dress (she kicked the toes of her shoes a little farther out, from under the hem of her dress) and carry a bouquet with flowers and ribbons

The ribbons stiffened in anticipation

and wear a summer hat with a big picture brim, and a spray of roses at the side.

The top of Alison's hat pushed up a little higher, hearing this

Alison stepped forward, excited. Again, they became as still as pictures in a book. Her Great Grandmother looked nervously around the room; she looked in Alison's direction, but she looked right through her. She didn't focus on Alison any more clearly than Alison could focus on her, straining to see through the glasses.

Then the people on the sofa whispered to each other, and as they spoke they grew dimmer.

The colored pencils Susan brought found themselves eager to spring into action to color them darker

The figures grew smaller. Smaller still. Alison pushed the glasses up and held them tightly against her nose. The man and woman no longer held hands; the man's hands were clasped, and the woman was touching the corner of her handkerchief to her eye. They were going out of focus, and no

30

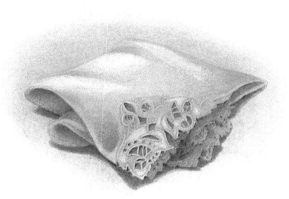

matter how hard she tried, Alison could hardly see them. They faded until they were gone, the two figures merging into one and narrowing into a column of smoke that rose and disappeared.

She looked at the lace curtains and could hardly see the pattern, the light outside was so dim. They were more like white sheets now, and as she looked back at the sofa, she saw no one, but heard whispered words (roses; the stars). She heard, again, the ticking of the clock.

She took off the glasses and put them in the box. It was almost completely dark in the room now. No shaft of light fell on the glasses. The lenses were dark as she put on the lid and turned to go to bed. The sofa was again a bed.

The bird cocked its head:

The colored pencils weren't going to redraw the scene to bring them back?

—"They've disappeared," the pencils said. "We can't draw all that from memory."

The clown — wouldn't the clown try to coax them out of hiding by doing a few tricks?

—The clown leaped up and did a somersault, keeping one hand on his hat. But when the clown swept off its hat to bow, there was no applause. The people had vanished from the sofa. The clown still bowed with dignity and walked away, with its floppy pink shoes going flip-flop in front of him. The shoes made such a breeze that the banners stirred.

—"Come on!" the banners said to the pencils. "Draw on us and we'll proclaim the wedding."

The pencils leaped into action and spelled out *Congratulations*.

The pink heart-shaped soaps liked the idea of a celebration so much that their heartbeats quickened in their box.

Alison smiled, and the bird sang a happy song. But the next time Alison looked, the bird was singing because it was dawn.

"GREAT GRANDMA," ALISON SAID the next afternoon, sitting on the bed, "tell me how Great Grandpa proposed."

"That was such a long time ago. It wasn't like now, when people have marriage contracts. They agree on who does what work and how the money will be divided if they get divorced."

"What did you and Great Grandpa agree about?"

"We didn't talk about everything, back then. And come to think of it, I'm sure that for years he and I never agreed on anything."

"Tell me what he said when he proposed."

"He said he loved me and wanted to marry me." Great Grandma lowered her head again; she turned it to one side, the way she had when he proposed.

"That was all?"

"That's all I remember," Great Grandma said, looking at Alison through her glasses, which were sliding down her nose.

"Did it surprise you when he asked?"

"I had some hint that he'd already asked my father. Men did that in those days. Now most men don't live in the same city as their fiancée's father. Anyway: I knew he was going to propose."

"You were sitting on a sofa when he asked, weren't you?"

"Yes," Great Grandmother said. "Did I already tell you this story?"

Alison's mother came into the bedroom and opened the curtains. She had sent Alison upstairs to awaken her Great Grandmother from her nap and to let the afternoon sunlight into the room, but Alison had started to ask questions and had forgotten to pull open the curtains.

A bird flew onto the window ledge and pecked at the glass. Alison's mother jumped, surprised.

"That bird must have seen its reflection," Great Grandmother said.

The bird ruffled its feathers as she spoke, flapped its wings, and was gone.

Great Grandmother shifted in bed, moving her head out of the sunlight. A little sun still struck the side of her glasses, though. Alison saw her Great Grandmother purse her lips. The light was annoying, no doubt. But as soon as Great Grandmother turned her head away, she turned it back into the light again. She was quiet for a while, and when she turned toward Alison she said, "Did you know that the sofa had a carved rose in the center, and the wood looked like fern, in a circle around it? And do you know what I was wearing when I was proposed to?"

Alison nodded.

"What?" Alison's mother said.

"Oh — a long dress. That was what I always wore." Great Grandmother shifted her head on the pillow. She said nothing for a few seconds, while part of her face was in the sun. Then she looked at Alison. "A dress that was pale yellow," she said, "with punchwork at the neck, and on the sleeves there were the prettiest little mother-of-pearl buttons, shaped like hearts. That turned out to be quite appropriate, didn't it?"

"You laughed when he asked?" Alison said.

Great Grandma squinted hard at her. "Why would I do that?" she said. She shifted on the bed again. "Well — I guess I did laugh a little."

"Because you were nervous?" Alison's mother said.

"I guess I was nervous."

"Why were you nervous, if you already knew?" Alison said.

"Because I couldn't imagine how things would turn out. It was going to change my life. And I wanted a different life, but —"

"But of course no one can predict the future," Alison's mother said.

"That's why it's fun to think about the past sometimes," Alison said. "And you don't always remember incorrectly. Sometimes you remember just the way it was."

"What *are* you talking about?" Alison's mother said.

"She's talking about the times things don't get in the way and everything is really wonderful instead of just remembered-wonderful," Great Grandmother said.

"Then what did you do — what happened when you said yes?" Alison said.

"Oh — there was a celebration. Later, not that night. I went to powder my face —" Great Grandmother sat up higher and looked out the window for a few seconds, then turned back toward Alison. "That's right . . . I had a compact shaped like a seashell. It was white and tan and had silver around the

35

rim. All the girls envied it. When I said yes, he went out and spoke to my parents and I went to powder my nose so I could gather my composure."

"And you had roses in the church for the wedding," Alison said.

"Pink and red," Great Grandmother said, turning her head to look right at Alison. "I see it all perfectly again," she said. "As if someone else looked back and reminded me of how it was."

ALISON'S MOTHER was in Alison's bedroom with her, helping to put away her birthday presents. She decided that the globe would fit onto the shelf of the bookcase. They both wondered if it would roll off. She folded the striped socks and put them in the top dresser drawer.

"Do you want these pretty soaps in there, so your clothes will smell nice until you want to use them?" Alison's mother said.

Alison nodded yes.

"I certainly hope you have a good memory, so you know who to thank for all these things," Alison's mother said.

Alison nodded yes again.

"Look at this," her mother said. "This belongs in the top drawer, too."

She was holding out a handkerchief, edged with lace, with small flowers embroidered in the center and tiny flowers in each corner.

"Who gave you this? It's absolutely beautiful."

"Don't worry," Alison said. "I remember."

Her mother put it gently in the drawer. "Be careful with this," she said. "It's valuable, I'm sure. You can tell that it's very old."

This book was set in Goudy Old Style and composed
by Accurate Typographers, Clearwater, Florida.
Printed and bound by R.R. Donnelley

Editor: Tom Durwood
Art Direction: Frazier Russell & Armand Eisen
Design: Barbara Bedick
Production: Wayne Kirn